Precipitations

Evelyn Scott

Alpha Editions

This edition published in 2024

ISBN 9789361478208

Design and Setting By

Alpha Editions

www.alphaedis.com

Email - info@alphaedis.com

MANHATTAN

THE UNPEOPLED CITY

MIDNIGHT WORSHIP: BROOKLYN BRIDGE

In the rain
Rows of street lamps are saints in bright garments
That flow long with the bend of knees.
They lift pale heads nimbussed with golden spikes.

Up the lanes of liquid onyx
Toward the high fire-laden altars
Move the saints of Manhattan
In endless pilgrimage to death,
Amidst the asphodel and anemones of dawn.

ASCENSION: AUTUMN DUSK IN CENTRAL PARK

Featureless people glide with dim motion through a quivering
    blue silver;
Boats merge with the bronze-gold welters about their keels.
The trees float upward in gray and green flames.
Clouds, swans, boats, trees, all gliding up a hillside
After some gray old women who lift their gaunt forms
From falling shrouds of leaves.

Thin fingered twigs clutch darkly at nothing.
Crackling skeletons shine.
Along the smutted horizon of Fifth Avenue
The hooded houses watch heavily
With oily gold eyes.

STARTLED FORESTS: HUDSON RIVER

The thin hill pushes against the mist.
Its fading defiance sounds in the umber and red of autumn leaves.
Like a dead arm around a warm throat
Is the sagging embrace of the river
Laid grayly about the shore.

The train passes.
We emerge from a tunnel into a sky of thin blue morning glories
Where yellow lily bells tinkle down.
The paths run swiftly away under the lamp glow

Like green and blue lizards
Mottled with light.

WINTER STREETS

The stars, escaping,
Evaporate in acrid mists.
The houses, rearing themselves higher,
Assemble among the clouds.
Night blows through me.
I am clear with its bitterness.
I tinkle along brick canyons
Like a crystal leaf.

FEBRUARY SPRINGTIME

The trees hold out pale gilded branches
Stiff and high in the wind.
On the lawns
Patches of gray-lilac snow
Melt in the hollows of the terraces.
The park is an ocean of fawn-colored plush,
Ridged and faded.
Sharp and delicate,
My shadow moves after me on the rumpled grass—
Grass like a pillow worn by a dear head.
Joy!

THE ASSUMPTION OF COLUMBINE

The lights trickle grayly down from the hoary palisades
And drip into the river.
Leaden reflections flow into the water.
Framed in your window,
Your little face glows deceptively
In a rigid ecstasy,
As the wide-winged morning
Folds back the mist.

FROM BROOKLYN

Along the shore
A black net of branches
Tangles the pulpy yellow lamps.
The shell-colored sky is lustrous with the fading sun.
Across the river Manhattan floats—
Dim gardens of fire—

And rushing invisible toward me through the fog,
A hurricane of faces.

SNOW DANCE

Black brooms of trees sweep the sky clean;
Sweep the house fronts,
And leave them bleak in sleep.
High up the empty moon
Spills her vacuity.

I dance.
My long black shadow

Weaves an invisible pattern of pain.
The snow
Is embroidered with my happiness.

POTTER'S FIELD

Golden petals, honey sweet,
Crushed beneath fear-hastened feet...

Silver paper lanterns glow and shudder
in flat patterns
On a gray eternal face
Stained with pain.

LIGHTS AT NIGHT

In the city,
Storms of light
Surge against the clouds,
Pushing up the darkness.

In the country,
Is the faint pressure of oil lamps,
That sputter,
Smothered with earth—
Extinguished in silence.

MIDNIGHT

The golden snow of the stars
Drifts in mounds of light,
Melts against the hot sides of the city,
Cool cheek against burning breast,
Cold golden snow,
Falling all night.

CROWDS

SUMMER NIGHT

The bloated moon
Has sickly leaves glistening against her
Like flies on a fat white face.

The thick-witted drunkard on the park bench
Touches a girl's breast
That throbs with its own ruthless and stupid delight.
The new-born child crawls in his mother's filth.
Life, the sleep walker,
Lifts toward the skies
An immense gesture of indecency.

NEW YORK

With huge diaphanous feet,
March the leaden velvet elephants,
Pressing the bodies back into the earth.

SUNSET: BATTERY PARK

From cliffs of houses,
Sunlit windows gaze down upon me
Like undeniable eyes,
Millions of bronze eyes,
Unassailable,
Obliterating all they see:
The warm contiguous crowd in the street below
Chills,
Mists,
Drifts past those hungry eyes of Eternity,
Melts seaward and deathward
To the ocean.

CROWDS

The sky along the street a gauzy yellow:
The narrow lights burn tall in the twilight.

The cool air sags,
Heavy with the thickness of bodies.
I am elated with bodies.
They have stolen me from myself.
I love the way they beat me to life,
Pay me for their cruelties.

In the close intimacy I feel for them
There is the indecency I like.

I belong to them,
To these whom I hate;
And because we can never know each other,
Or be anything to each other,
Though we have been the most,
I sell so much of me that could bring a better price.

RIOTS

As if all the birds rushed up in the air,
Fluttering;
Hoots, calls, cries.
I never knew such a monster even in child dreams.

It grows:
Glass smashed;
Stores shut;
Windows tight closed;
Dull, far-off murmurs of voices.

Blood—
The soft, sticky patter of falling drops in the silence.
Everything inundated.
Faces float off in a red dream.
Still the song of the sweet succulent patter.

Blood—
I think it oozes from my finger tips.
—Or maybe it drips from the brow of Jesus.

THE CITY AT NIGHT

Life wriggles in and out
Through the narrow ways
And circuitous passages:
Something monstrous and horrible,
A passion without any master,
Male sexual fluid trickling through the darkness
And setting fire to whatever it touches.

That is the master
Bestowing a casual caress on a slave.
Quiver under it!

VANITIES

BREAD POEMS

LULLABY

I lean my heart against the soft bosomed night:
A white globed breast,
And warm and silent flowing,
The milk of the moon.

EMBARKATION OF CYTHERA

Like jellied flowers
My inflated curves
Melt in the peaceful stagnance of the bath.
If I were to die
I would resist the final agony
With only a faint quiver
From my escaping thighs.

CHRISTIAN LUXURIES

The red fountain of shame gushes up from my heart.
I throw back my long hair and the fountain floats it out
Like a fiery fan.
My wide stretched arms are white coral branches.
The liquid shadows seek between my amber breasts.

But the fire is cool.
It cannot burn me.

NARROW FLOWERS

I am a gray lily.
My roots are deep.
I cannot lift my hands
For one thin yellow butterfly.
Yet last night I grew up to a star.
My shade swirled mistily
Seven mountains high.
I lifted my face to another face.
The moon made a burning shadow on my brow.
Washed by the light,
My sharp breasts silvered.
My dance was an arc of mist
From west to east.

EYES

There are arms of ice around me,
And a hand of ice on my heart.
If they should come to bury me
I would not flinch or start.
For eyes are freezing me—
Eyes too cold for hate.
I think the ground,
Because it is dark,
A warmer place to wait.

AFTER YOUTH

Oh, that mysterious singing sadness of youth!
Exotic colors in the lamplit darkness of wet streets,
Musk and roses in the twilight,
The moon in the park like a golden balloon…

Then to awaken and find the shadows fled,
The music gone…
Empty, bleak!
My soul has grown very small and shriveled in my body.
It no longer looks out.
It rattles around,
And inside my body it begins to look,
Staring all around inside my body,
Like a crab in a crevice,
Staring with bulging eyes
At the strange place in which it finds itself.

THE SHADOW THAT WALKS ALONE

The silence tugs at my breast
With formless lips,
Like a heavy baby,
Attenuates me,
Draws me through myself into it.
I sit in the womb of an idiot,
Helpless before its mouthing tenderness.
The huge flap ears are attentive,
And the soundless face bends toward me
In horrible lovingness.

BIBLE TRUTH

To die…
Oh, cool river!
To float there with nothing to resist—

One ripple of silence spreads out from another.
My spirit widens so,
Circle beyond circle.
I hold up the stars no longer with the pupils of my eyes.
Hands, legs, arms float off from me.
I melt like flakes of snow.

I am no more opposed.
I am no more.

THE MATERNAL BREAST

I walked straight and long,
But I never found you.
I was looking for a hill of a hundred breasts,
A hill modeled after the statues of Diana of the Ephesians.
I was looking for a hill of mounds hairy with grass,
And a place to lie down.

AIR FOR G STRING

White hands of God
With fingers like strong twigs flowering
Rock me in leaves of iron,
Leaves of blue.

Hands of God
Fashioned of clouds
Have finger tips that balance the almond white moon.
The pale sky is a flower
White tipped and pink tipped with dawn.
White hands of God gather the blossoms with fingers that hold me,
Cloud fingers like milk in the azure night,
Weaving strong chords.

DESTINY

I am lost in the vast cave of night.
No sound but the far-off tinkle of stars,
And the cry of a bird
Muffled in shadows.

The light flows in remotely
Through the hollow moon,
Dim strange brilliance
From waters beyond the sky.
Groping,
I listen to the harsh tinkle of the far-off stars,
Feel the clammy shadows about my shoulders.

THE RED CROSS

HECTIC

I

Ruby winged pains flash through me,
Jewel winged agonies:
They vanish,
Carrying me with them
Without my knowing it.

II

Pain sends out long tentacles
And sucks.
When I have given up struggling
He takes me into his arms.

ISOLATION WARD

We are the separate centers of consciousness
Of all the universes.
We vibrate statically on a trillion golden wires.
Our trillion golden fingers twine in the weltering darkness,
And grasp tremblingly,
Aware in agony
Of the things we can never know.

THE RED CROSS

Antiseptic smells that corrode the nostrils
Crumble me,
Eat me deep;
And my garments disintegrate:
First my nightgown,
Leaving my naked arms and legs disjointed,
Sprawled about the bed in postures meaningless to the point of
    obscenity.

My breasts shrivel,
The nipples drawn like withered plums
To the eyes of the bright young nurse.
I am nothing but a dull eye myself,
An eye out of a socket,
Bursting,
Contorted with hideous wisdom.

Eye to eye
We fight in the death throes,
Myself and the young nurse.
Her firm, crisp aproned bosom
Leans toward the bed,
As she smooths the rumpled pillow back
With long cool fingers.

HOSPITAL NIGHT

I am Will-o'-the-Wisp.
I float in a little pool of delirium,
Phosphorescent velvet.
My fire is like a breath
That blows my illness in circles,
Widening it so far
That I cannot see the edge.
It is one with the night sky.
My fire has blown this vastness,
But I strain and flicker trying to escape from it.
I want to exist without the darkness
That makes my breath so bright.
I want the morning to thin my light.

DOMESTIC CANTICLE

SPRING SONG

Sap crashes suddenly through dead roots:
Sap that bites,
Harsh,
Impatient,
Bitter as gold.

My God, my sisters, how dark, how silent, how heavy is earth!
Shoulders strain against this eternity,
Against the trickling loam.
Earth dropped on the heart like a nerveless hand:
On the red mouth

Earth coils,
Heavy as a serpent.
Light has come back to the darkness,
To the shadow,
To the coolness of blackened leaves.

HOME AGAIN

Where I used to be
I could hear the sea.
The black ragged palm fronds flung themselves against
     the twilight sky.
The moon stared up from the water like a fish's eye.
I had the loneliness that sings.
It made me light and gave me wings.

Is it the dust and the iron railings and the blank red brick
That makes me sick?
There is no space to be lonely any more
And crumbling feet on a city street
Sound past the door.

TO A SICK CHILD

At the end of the day
The sun rusts.
The street is old and quiet.
The houses are of iron.
The shadows are iron.
Shrill screams of children scrape the iron sky.
Let us lock ourselves in the light.
Let the sun nail us to the hot earth with his spikes of fire,
And perhaps when the darkness rushes past
It will forget us.

LOVE SONG

(To C. K. S.)

Little father,
Little mother,
Little sister,
Little brother,
Little lover,
How can I go on living
With you away from me?

How can I get up in the morning
And go to bed at night,
And you not here?
How can I bear the sunrise and the sunset,
And the moonrise and the moonset,
And the flowers in the garden?

How can I bear them,
You,
My little father,
Little mother,
Little sister,
Little brother,
Little lover?

QUARREL

Abruptly, from a wall of clear cold silence
Like an icy glass,
Myself looked out at me
And would not let me pass.
I wanted to reach you
Before it was too late;
But my frozen image barred the way
With vacant hate.

MY CHILD

Tentacles thrust imperceptibly into the future
Helplessly sense the fire.
A serpentine nerve
Impelled to lengthen itself generation after generation
Pierces the labyrinth of flames
To rose-colored extinction.

THE TUNNEL

I

I have made you a child in the womb,
Holding you in sweet and final darkness.
All day as I walk out
I carry you about.
I guard you close in secret where
Cold eyed people cannot stare.
I am melted in the warm dear fire,
Lover and mother in the same desire.

Yet I am afraid of your eyes
And their possible surprise.
Would you be angry if I let you know
That I carried you so?

II

I could kiss you to death
Hoping that, your protest obliterated,
You would be
Utterly me.
Yet I know—how well!—
Like a shell,
Hollow and echoing,
Death would be,
With a roar of the past
Like the roar of the sea.
And what is lifeless I cannot kill!
So you would make death work your will.

III

In most intimate touch we meet,
Lip to lip,
Breast to breast,
Sweet.
Suddenly we draw apart
And start.
Like strangers surprised at a road's turning
We see,
I, the naked you;
You, the naked me.
There was something of neither of us
That covered the hours,
And we have only touched each other's bodies
Through veils of flowers.
But let us smile kindly,
Like those already dead,
On the warm flesh
And the marriage bed.

IV

The blanched stars are withered with light.
The moon is pale with trying to remember something.

Light, straining for a stale birth,
Distends the darkness.

I, in the midst of this travail,
Bring forth—
The solitude is so vast
I am glad to be freed of it.
Is it the moon I see there,
Or does my own white face
Hang in blank agony against the sky
As if blinded with giving?

V

Little inexorable lips at my breast
Drink me out of me
In a fine sharp stream.
Little hands tear me apart
To find what they need.

I am weak with love of you,
Little body of hate!

BRUISED SUNLIGHT

WATER MOODS

RAIN ON THE SEASHORE

Curling petals of rain lick silver tongues.
Fluffy spray is blown loosely up between thin silver lips
And slithers, tinkling in hard green ice, down the gray rocks.

White darkness—
An expressionless horizon stares with stone eyes.
The sea lifts its immense self heavily
And falls down in sickly might.

The emptiness is like a death of which no one shall ever know.

SHIP MASTS

They stand
Stark as church spires;
Bare stalks
That will blossom
(Tomorrow perhaps)
Into flowers of the wind.

MONOCHROME

Gray water,
Gray sky drifting down to the sea.
The night,
Old, ugly, and stern,
Lies upon the water,
Quivering in the twilight
Like a tortured belly.

ANTIQUE

Clouds flung back
Make fan-shaped rays of faded crimson
Brocaded on dim blue satin;
Through the wrinkled dust-blue water
The little boat
Glides above its sunken shadow.

ECHO LOOKS AT HERSELF

The ship passes in the night
And drags jagged reflections
Like gilded combs
Through the obscure water.
Spun glass daisies float on a gold-washed mirror.

SPELL

In the dark I can hear the patter.
Bare white feet are running across the water.
White feet as bright as silver
Are flashing under dull blue dresses.
Wet palms beat,
Impatiently,
Petulantly,
Slapping the wet rocks.

HUNGRY SHADOWS

RAINY TWILIGHT

Dim gold faces float in the windows.
Dim gold faces and gilded arms…
They are clinging along the silver ladders of rain;
They are climbing with ivory lamps held high,
Starry lamps

Over which the silver ladders
Thicken into nets of twilight.

THE STORM

Herds of black elephants,
Rushing over the plains,
Trample the stars.
The ivory tusk of the leader
(Or is it the moon?)
Flashes, and is gone.
Tree tops bend;
Crash;
Fire from hoofs;
And still they rush on,
Trampling the stars,
Bellowing,
Roaring.

NYMPHS

The drift of shadows on the mountainside,
Blue and purple gold!
Purple dust sifting through fingers of ivory:
Cool purple on ivory breasts.
I see arms and breasts,
Upturned chins,
Slanting through the dust of purple leaves:
Ivory and gold,
Bare breasts and laughing eyes,
That drift on the shadowy surf
And surge against the side of the mountain.

WINTER DAWN

Cloudy dawn flower unfolds;
Moon moth gyrates slowly;
Snow maiden lets down her hair,
And in one shining silence,
It slips to earth.

THE WALL OF NIGHT

SPRINGTIME TOO SOON

The moon is a cool rose in a blue bowl.
There are no more birds.

The last leaf has fallen.
The trees in the twilight are naked old women.

The moon is an old woman at the door of her tomb.
Clouds combed out in the wind
Are gray hair she has wound about her neck.
The water is an old gray face that mirrors the springtime.

STARS

Like naked maidens
Dancing with no thought of lovers,
Blinking stars with dewy silver breasts
Pass through the darkness.
White and eager,
They glide on
Toward the gray meshed web of dawn

And the mystery of morning.
Then,
About me,
The white cloud walls
Stand as sternly as sepulchers,
And from all sides
Peer and linger the startled faces,
Pale in the harshness of the sunlight.

NIGHT MUSIC

Through the blue water of night
Rises the white bubble of silence—
Rises,
And breaks:
The shivered crystal bell of the moon,
Dying away in star splinters.
The still mists bear the sound
Beyond the horizon.

NOCTURNE OF WATER

A shining bird plunges to the deep,
Becomes entangled with seaweed,
And never more emerges.
Pale golden feathers drift across the sky,
Fire feathered clouds,
Riding the weightless billows of back velvet
On the horizon.

THE LONG MOMENT

A white sigh clouds the fields
Into quietness.
Above the billowed snow
I drift,
One year,
Two years,
Three years.
Hurt eyes mist in the blue behind me.
The moon uncoils in glistening ropes
And I glide downward along the dripping rays
To a marble lake.

DESIGNS

I

Night

Fields of black tulips
And swarms of gold bees
Drinking their bitter honey.

II

New Moon

Above the gnarled old tree
That clings to the bleakest side of the mountain,
A torch of ivory and gold;
And across the sky,
The silver print
Of spirit feet,
Fled from the wonder.

III

Tropic Moon

The glowing anvil,
Beaten by the winds;
Star sparks,
Burning and dying in the heavens;
The furnace glare
Red
On the polished palm leaves.

IV

Winter Moon

> A little white thistle moon
> Blown over the cold crags and fens:
> A little white thistle moon
> Blown across the frozen heather.

ARGO

> White sails
> Unbillowed by any wind,
> The moon ship,
> Among shoals of cloud,
> Stranded stars,
> Bare bosoms,
> And netted hair of light,
> On the shores of the world.

JAPANESE MOON

> Thick clustered wistaria clouds,
> A young girl moon in a mist of almond flowers,
> Boughs and boughs of light;
> Then a round-faced ivory lady
> Nodding among fading chrysanthemums.

HOT MOON

> Moon rise.
> Great gong sounds, shining—
> Little feet run away.
> Loud and solemn, the funeral gong.
> Little feet run away.

THE NAIAD

> The moon rises,
> Glistening,
> Naked white,
> Out of her stream.
>
> Wet marble shoulders
> Shake star drops on the clouds.

FLOODTIDE

> Across the shadows of the surf
> The lights of the ship

Twinkle despondently.
The clinging absorbent gray darkness
Sucks them into itself:
Drinks the pale golden tears greedily.

MOUNTAIN PASS IN AUGUST

Night scatters grapes for the harvest.
The moon burns like a leaf.
Along the mountain path
A thin streak of light
Creeps hungrily with its silver belly to the earth.
The old hound laps up the shadows.
Her teats drip the brighter darkness.

CONTEMPORARIES

HARMONICS

YOUNG MEN

Fauns,
Eternal pagans,
Beautiful and obscene,
Leaping through the street
With a flicker of hoofs,
And a flash of tails,

You want dryads
And they give you prostitutes.

YOUNG GIRLS

Your souls are wet flowers,
Bathed in kisses and blood.
Golden Clyties,
The wheel of light
Rushes over your breasts.

HOUSE SPIRITS

Women are flitting around in their shells.
Pale dilutions of the waters of the world
Come through the windows.
Back and forth the women glide in their little waters;
Cellar to garret and garret to cellar,
Winding in and out under door arches and down passages,
They and their spawn,

In the shell,
In the cavern.

You may come in the shell to overpower her,
Males,
But in the shell, in the shell.
She cannot be torn from the shell without dying;
And what is the pleasure of intercourse with the dead?

AT THE MEETING HOUSE

Souls as dry as autumn leaves,
The color long since out.

The organ plays.
The leaves crackle and rustle a little;
Then sink down.

Old ladies with gray moss on their chins,
Old men with camphor and cotton packed around their heads,
Thin child spirits, sharp and shrill as whistles.

Gray old trees;
Gaunt old woods;
Souls as dry as leaves
After autumn is past.

CHRISTIANS

Blind, they storm up from the pit.
You gave them the force,
You, when You poured the measure of agony into them.
Didn't You know what it would be,
Giving blind people fire?
Not gold and red and amber fire,
But marsh fire.
Fire of ice,
Suffering forged into suffering!

They are coming up now.
The sword is uplifted in the hands of the monster.

My valiant little puppets,
Did you think you could stand out against this?
Pierrot and Columbine breeding in the flowers....

There must be no flowers.

DEVIL'S CRADLE

Black man hanged on a silver tree;
(Down by the river,
Slow river,
White breast,
White face with blood on it.)
Black man creaks in the wind,
Knees slack.
Brown poppies, melting in moonlight,
Swerve on glistening stems
Across an endless field
To the music of a blood white face
And a tired little devil child
Rocked to sleep on a rope.

WOMEN

Crystal columns,
When they bend they crack;
Brittle souls,
Conforming, yet not conforming—
Mirrors.

Masculine souls pass across the mirrors:
Whirling, gliding ecstasies—
Retreating, retreating,
Dimly, dimly,
Like dreams fading across the mirrors.

Then the mirrors,
Stark and brilliant in the sunshine,
Blank as the desert,
Blank as the Sphinx,
Winking golden eyes in the twinkles of light,
Silent, immutable, vacuous infinity,
Illimitable capacity for absorption,
Absorbing nothing.

Have the shapes and the shadows been swallowed up
In your recesses without depth,
You drinkers of life,
Twinkling maliciously
Your golden yellow eyes,
Mirrors winking in the sunshine?

PENELOPE

Gray old spinners,
Weaving with the crafty fibers of your souls;
Nothing was given you but those impalpable threads.

Yet you have bound the race,
Stranglers,
With your silver spun mysteries.
All the cruel,
All the mad,
The foolish,
And the beautiful, too:
It all belongs to you
Since the first time
That you began to drop the filmy threads
When the world was half asleep.

Sometimes you are young girls;
Sometimes there are roses in your hair.
But I know you—
Sitting back there in the hollow shadows of your wombs.
The crafty fibers of your souls
Are woven in and out
With the fibers of life.

POOR PEOPLE'S DREAMS

Sometimes women with eyes like wet green berries
Glide across the slick mirror of their own smiles
And vanish through lengths of gold and marble drawing rooms.
The marble smiles,
As sensuous as snow;
Hips of the Graces;

Shoulders of Clytie;
Breasts frozen as foam,
Frozen as camelia bloom;
Mounds of marble flesh,
Inexplicable wonder of white....

I dream about statuesque beauties
Who look from the shadows of opera boxes;
Or elegant ladies in novels of eighteen thirty,
At the hunt ball...
Reflections in a polish floor,
A portrait by Renoir,

A Degas dancing girl,
English country houses,
An autumn afternoon in the Bois,
Something I have read of…
In sleep one vision retreating through another,
Like mirrors being doors to other mirrors,
Satin, and lace, and white shoulders,
And elegant ladies,
Dancing, dancing.

FOR WIVES AND MISTRESSES

Death,
Being a woman,
Being passive like all final things,
Being a mother,
Waits.

Shining faces
Gray and melt into her flesh.
Death envies those asleep in her,
Little children who have come back,
Fiery faces,
Bright for a moment in the darkness,
Extinguished softly in her womb.

PORTRAITS

PORTRAIT OF RICH OLD LADY

Old lady talks,
Spins from her lips
Warp and woof
Of teapots, tables, napery,
Sanitary toilets,
Old bedsteads, pictures on walls,
And fine lace,
Spins a cocoon of this secondary life.

Warm and snug is old lady's belly.
Old lady makes Venus Aphrodite
Parvenue.
Old lady
Arranges places for courtesans
In warm outbuildings on back streets.

NIGGER

Nigger with flat cheeks and swollen purple lips;
Nigger with loose red tongue;
Flat browed nigger,
Your skull peaked at the zenith,
The stretched glistening skin
Covered with tight coiled springs of hair:
I am up here cold.
I am white man.
You are still warm and sweet
With the darkness you were born in.

THE MAIDEN MOTHER

He has a squat body,
Glowering brows,
And bulging eyes.
Lustful contemplation of the meat pie
Is written all over his sweating face.

The thin woman with the meek voice,
Who has carried him so long in her body
And despairs of giving him birth,
Watches over him in secret
With bitter and resentful tenderness.

A PIOUS WOMAN

You can bury your face in her thick soul of cotton batting
And smell candle wax and church incense.
When she dies she must be burned.
Laid in the ground she would only soak up moisture
And get soggy,
As now she has a way of soaking up tears
Never meant for her.

A VERY OLD ROSE JAR

She ran across the lawn after the cat
And I saw through the old maid, as through a shadow,
A young girl in a white muslin dress running to meet her lover.
There was clashing of cymbals,
And the flash of nereids' arms in autumn leaves.
A sharp high note died out like an ascending light.
Something sweet and wanton faded from the old maid's lips—

Something of Pierrot chasing after love,
A bacchante dying in her sleep,
A shadow,
And a gray cat.

THE NIXIE

He lies in cool shadows safe under rocks,
His eyes brown stones,
Worn smooth and soft,
But uncrumbled.
He reaches forth covert child-claws
To tickle the silver bellies of the little blind fish
As they swim secretly above him.
He laughs—
The school splinters, panic stricken.

As we stare through the lucid gold water
He gazes up at us from his shadowy retreat
In combative safety.
There are times when he pretends to himself that he is a god,
Water god, land god, god-in-the-sky.
We cannot laugh at his grotesquerie.
We are wistful before the pathetic gallantries of his
    imagination.

OLD LADIES' VALHALLA

I am thinking of a little house,
A pretty gray silk dress,
And a little maid with a tidy white apron.

I am thinking of thin yellow angels
Flying out of Sevres china tea cups,
And a cool spirit with slanting green eyes,
Who peers at me through the screen of plants
I have placed in the corner between the hearth and the window.
I am thinking of the peace in one's own little home
When the afternoon sunshine drips on the shiny floor,
And the rugs are in order,
And the roses in the bowl plunge into shadow
Like pink nymphs into a pool,
While there is no sound to be heard above the hum
    of the teakettle
Save the benevolent buzzing of flies in the clean sash curtain.

PORTRAITS OF POETS

I

(For L. R.)

To rush over dark waters,
A swift bird with cruel talons;
To seize life—
Your life for her—
To hold it,
Hold it struggling—
To kiss it.

II

Crystal self-containment,
Giving out only what is sent.
Startled,
The circumference retreats
As it mounts higher, flamelike,
Still and clear without radiance,
Ascending without self-explanation.

A skeleton falls apart
With the dignity of comprehensible pathos,
The bones bleached by denial.

III

With the impalpable lightness of May breezes
Begins a battle of flower petals:
Cowering in the primrose whirlwind his lips have blown,
The little grotesque with the shattered heart,
Fearful,
Yet sinister in his fearfulness.

THEODORE DREISER

The man body jumbled out of the earth, half formed,
Clay on the feet,
Heavy with the lingering might of chaos.
The man face so high above the feet
As if lonesome for them like a child.
The veins that beat heavily with the music they but half
    understood
Coil languidly around the heart
And lave it in the death stream
Of a grand impersonal benignance.

PIETA

The child—
Warm chubby thighs,
Fat brown arms,
An unsurprised face—
Cries for jam.
The mother buys him with jam.

An old woman,
Tottering on lean leather skinned legs,
Sucks with glazing eyes
The crystal silken milk
That flows from the death wound
In a young flower-soft, jewel-soft body.

BRAZIL THROUGH A MIST

THE RANCH

TROPICAL LIFE

White flower,
Your petals float away
But I hardly hear them.

TWENTY-FOUR HOURS

The day is so long and white,
A road all dust,
Smooth monotony;
And the night at the end,
A hill to be climbed,
Slowly, laboriously,
While the stars prick our hands
Like thistles.

RAINY SEASON

A flock of parrakeets
Hurled itself through the mist;
Harsh wild green
And clamor-tongued
Through the dim white forest.
They vanished,
And the lips of Silence
Sucked at the roots of Life.

MAIL ON THE RANCH

The old man on the mule
Opens the worn saddle bags,
And takes out the papers.

From the outer world
The thoughts come stabbing,
To taunt, baffle, and stir me to revolt.
I beat against the sky,
Against the winds of the mountain,
But my cries, grown thin in all this space,
Are diluted with emptiness…
Like the air,
Thin and wide,
Touching everything,
Touching nothing.

THE VAMPIRE BAT

What was it that came out of the night?
What was it that went away in the night?
The little brown hen is huddled in the fence corner,
Eyes already glazing.
How should she know what came out of the night,
Or what was taken away in the night?
A shadow passed across the moon.
The wind rustled in the mango trees.
And now, in the morning,
The little brown hen is huddled in the fence corner,
Eyes already glazing;
Because a shadow passed across the moon,
And the wind rustled in the mango trees.

CONSERVATISM

The turkeys,
Like hoop-skirted old ladies
Out walking,
Display their solemn propriety.

A terrible force,
Hungry and destructive,
Emanates from their mistily blinking eyes.

LITTLE PIGS

Little tail quivering,
Wrinkled snout thrusting up the mud:
He will find God
If he keeps on like that.

THE SILLY EWE

The silly ewe comes smelling up to me.
Her tail wriggles without hinges,
Both ends of it at once and equal.
Yesterday the parrot bit her;
Last week the jaguar ate her young one;
But experience teaches her nothing.

THE SNAKE

The chickens are at home in the barnyard,
The pigs in the swill,
And the flowers in the garden;
But where do you belong,
With your lacquered coils,
O snake?

THE YEAR

Days and days float by.
On the sides of the mountains
Blue shadows shift
And sift into silence.
Morning...
The cock crows.
There is that rosy glow on the mountain's edge;
Jose in the door of his hut;
Maria's lace bobbins
Tapping, tapping.
Evening...
The parrot's shrill cry;
Pale silver green stars.
Night...
The ghosts of dead Joses
And dead Marias
Sitting in the moonlight.
Peace—
Depressing,
Interminable
Peace.

BURNING MOUNTAINS

I

A herder set fire to the grass
On the other side of the valley,
And now a beautiful Indian woman
Bends, whirls, undulates,
Tosses her gold braceleted arms into the air—
Then sinks into her gray veil.

II

Fire, dying in smoke,
You stir behind the haze
Like a warrior
Who threatens in his sleep.

VILLA NOVA DA SERRA

The mountains are as dull and sodden
As drunkards' faces,
And the white forgetfulness of rain
Is like a delirium.
Along the filthy crooked streets of the little town,
Street lamps float in pools of mist—
The eyes of children being beaten.

RAIN IN THE MOUNTAINS

Like inexorable peace,
The mists march through the mountains.
One by one the grim peaks sink into the cold arms
    of the unspoken.
The little town with the pink and white houses
Looses its hold on the ridge of hills
And floats among cloud tops.
A shaggy donkey, cropping grass in the sequestered church yard,
Walks, with a leisurely air,
Into a wind driven abyss.

TROPICAL WINTER

The afternoon is frozen with memories,
Radiant as ice.
The sun sets amidst the agued trembling of the leaves,
Sinking right down through the gold air

Into the arms of the sea.
The enameled wings of the palm trees
Keep shivering, shivering,
Beating the gold air thin….

TALK ON THE RANCH

It is cold in the circle of mountains,
A fireless hearth.
The stars drift by like autumn leaves.
Only the rustle—
Then, close together,
Our talk,
For and counter,
One grating against the other,
Rubs a little fire
And we warm each other
There in the midst of the hollow clammy circle.

LES MALADIES DES PAYS CHAUDS

PRIDE OF RACE

I saw his young Anglo-Saxon form
In its white sailor clothes
Cleave through the scampering yellow Latin crowd,
As white and clean as the blade of an archangel;
And, as he reeled along, gloriously drunk,
Those little black and gold dung beetles
Seemed to be pushing and racing over his body.

DON QUIXOTE SOJOURNS IN RIO DE JANEIRO

White roses climb the wall of night.
A pale face looks from a window in the sky.
O Moon, is it because you have seen her that you are beautiful?
Is she happy among the saints?
I placed white flowers in the coffin.
Are they the blossoms that lie scattered along the horizon,
Tangled in your light?
Dim stars drop into the sea.
So you give my flowers back to me, do you, Bella Dona?
I might gather the petals and carry them to Antonietta to trim
    her hats.
So much for life with a little negro milliner
In the Rua Chile!

CONVENT MUSINGS

Eleven thousand white-faced virgins in the sky.
The eyes of Our Lady
Smiling through a rift of cloud.

I see Sister Maria da Gloria's fat shadow
Pass across the whitewashed wall by the window....

Eleven thousand white-faced virgins—
Stars from a broken rosary—
The Southern Cross—
Thrum, thrum, my fingers on the bench.
I sometimes think of God
As an enormous emptiness
Into which we must all enter at last,
Our Lady forgive me.

GUITARRA

"An orange tree without fruit,
So am I without loves,"
His heavy lidded eyes sang up to her.
Her glance dropped on her golden globe of breast,
And on the baby.

NOVEMBER

Foreign sailors in the streets
Are as sad a sight as wild geese in the winter—

There was one boy with those strange young blue eyes
Who looked at me;
And a long, long time after he had passed
The light of his soul got to me—
So long on the way—
Like the light of a dead star.

What makes you look so lonesome, Blue Eyes?

THE COMING OF CHRIST

THE DEATH OF COLUMBINE

DUET

Pierrot sings.
The moon, a clown like himself,
Stares down upon him
With vacuous tenderness.

For a moment the night is filled with rice powder
And spangled gauze.
Then two shades embracing each other
Find in their arms
Only the darkness.

FROM A MAN DYING ON A CROSS

The pains in my palms are threads of sightless fire
Drawn like fiery veins through blackened marble walls,
Crashing with a dull roar
To the ends of the earth.

Winey peace....
My sick blood purrs.
Milky bosoms float through red hair,
Gaunt faces and sick eyes
Beside her face.
I debauch them with my forgiveness.
Only her, I cannot forgive.

Moonlight trembles as the silk of her garment,
Perfumed silk.
The cross makes a long harsh shadow
Rigid on the sand.
Her white feet stir across the shadow.

LAGNIAPPE

You in the quiet garden,
You with the death sweet smile,
Before you speak of love to me
Go out and hate awhile.

The kind devil
Has a tolerant grin.
He flings the golden gates out wide
And lets poor people in.
He warms them in his bosom
And guards their pain.
He shows them hell fields that are bright
And skies gentle with rain.

But up in paradise
The stern Lord is wise,
And Michael with his flaming sword
Puts out the angels' eyes.

HAIL MARY!

Pierrette is dead!
Between her narrow little breasts
They have laid a cross of lead.
Her tight pale lips are sunken.
Her fleshless fingers clutch the pall.
Why did she have to die like that,
And she so small?

THE DEATH OF COLUMBINE

White breast beaten in sea waves,
Hair tangled in foam,
Lonely sky,
Desolate horizon,
Pale and shining clouds:
All this desolate and shining sea is no place for you,
My dead Columbine.

And the waves will bite your breast;
And the wind, that does not know death from life,
Will leap upon you and leer into your eyes
And suck at your dead lips.

Oh, my little Columbine,
You go farther and farther away from me,
Out where there are no ships
And the solemn clouds
Soar across the somber horizon.

PIERROT LAUGHS

You are old, Pierrot,
But I do not laugh
As in harlequinade
You totter down the path.
Now you are old, Pierrot,
And drool to your guitar,
I do not cast you off.
Though your love songs are as feeble as a winter fly's
I do not scoff.
Exultant
I cast back on you
What you gave me,
And bind you with the unasked love
That has kept me from being free!

THE TRANSMIGRATION OF CALIBAN

Once I had a little brother,
An ugly little brother that was I.
I was still in the nursery
When they nailed him to a clean white cross,
And said he was dead.
He flapped there all day,
Thin and stiff as a jumping jack.

But when I had gone to bed,
And the lights were out,
And the muslin curtains rustled in white secrecy,
And through the thin brown glass like onion skin
I could see the bright moon sag to the tree tops
With a heaviness I dimly understood,
While the haggard branches gauntly strained,
As useless to the moon as she to them,
I was rocked in an orange and umber cradle,
A rosy bubble light with fireshine
Floating atop the cold,
And my little brother was burning merrily,
His twisted figure
A writhing grotesque.

Yet his face never moved
And never burnt up.
And when I had drifted asleep
I still saw it
Like a reflection trapped in a mirror.
And I couldn't brush it out!
I couldn't brush it out!

GUNDRY

There are little blood flecks on the snow.
There is blood in the heart of the white hyacinth.
I saw her pale body harsh as a flash of lightning
Between the gray torsos of the trees.
She had a little child.
She held a little child in her breast.
She went quickly through the dim forest.
I have seen her feet.
They are as white as ivory.
Where she ran there are little red tracks.
And it is not yet springtime!

VIENNESE WALTZ

Dresden china shepherdesses
Whirl in the silver sunshine:
Columbine stars
Float in gauze petticoats of light....
Little Columbine ghosts, wrinkled and old,
Smelling of jasmine and camphor:
Prim arms folded over immaculate breasts....

The pirouetting tune dies....
Stars and little faded faces,
Waltzing, waltzing,
Shoot slowly downward
On tinkling music,
Dusty little flowers
Sinking into oblivion.

After the music,
Quiet,
The glacial period renewed,
Monsters on earth,
A mad conflagration of worlds on ardent nights—

These too vanishing—
Silence unending.

RESURRECTION

IMMORTALITY

Death is a child of stone.
Death is a little white stone goat.
The little goat child dances motionless.
Little kid feet make a circle around the world:
Bas-relief of Death,
Little stone goats capering across the clouds.

Perhaps Death is nearest in the spring.
Then Her flower clouds the woods with white blossoms,
Apple blossoms, quince blossoms,
Pear snow.
These are the flowers that drift in the hair of the dead.
The sun shines on stone eyelids
That melt with light.
This smile is a pale happiness;
It glows motionless

On the rocky hillside and the long stems of trees.
There are no shadows in this happy light:
The glow beat by little goat hoofs
Chiseled across the clouds in motionless delight,
While suns fade behind crumbling hillsides
And hungry illusions vanish
In generation after generation.

AUTUMN NIGHT

The moon is as complacent as a frog.
She sits in the sky like a blind white stone,
And does not even see Love
As she caresses his face with her contemptuous light.
She reaches her long white shivering fingers
Into the bowels of men.
Her tender superfluous probing into all that pollutes
Is like the immodesty of the mad.
She is a mad woman holding up her dress
So that her white belly shines.
Haughty,
Impregnable,
Ridiculous,
Silent and white as a debauched queen,
Her ecstasy is that of a cold and sensual child.

She is Death enjoying Life,
Innocently,
Lasciviously.

VENUS' FLY TRAP

A wax bubble moon trembles on the honey-blue horizon.
Softly heated by your breast
Pearl wax languorously unfolds her lily lips of mist,
Swells about you,
Weaves you into herself through each moist pore,
Absorbs you deliciously,
Destroys you.

SUICIDE

A dirty little beetle
Peers into motionless eyes
Transfixed to their depths
As by shining needles.
Limbs are taut in ultimate resentment.

A bare sky confronts an upturned face.
Like a wheel vanishing in speed
The corpse, containing everything,
Has swallowed itself.

LEAVES

I

The women hold a child up for a shield,
And speak of it tenderly,
Seeing it bloody.

II

The lovers throw back the scented coverlet
And are afraid.
Seeing Death in their own nakedness,
They shroud it with flowers.

III

The corpse was stiff like an arrow.
As they carried it past the onlookers
It pierced the crowd with its life.
Blank white faces floated back
In terror of its vividness.

IV

The man was dead.
It was seen to that he was buried.
Again and again they dug the bones up,
But when they could no longer find the bones
They groped for the proof of death
In fear of the resurrection.

ALLEGRO

(At the Cemetery)

The mounds stir in the sunshine.
Bones clack a light staccato.
Bare wrist bones,
Thigh bones,
Ankle bones,
Kick the soil loose.

Moldy draperies flutter back and forth through the light.
The trees have put on a thin green pretense.

Even the soil pretends to fecundity.
Toothless jaws widen in a smile of real mirth.
Bones lightened of flesh
Flash in the sunshine.

And afterward
The dead rest in the spring night,
Each in a silence molded to him,
Each in his own night,
A casket with a spangled lining.
The dead rest deep in their happiness.

Milton Keynes UK
Ingram Content Group UK Ltd.
UKHW050243220624
444555UK00005BA/501